The Tale of the
Border Knight

A. R. Witham

Nepenthe House

For Andrew,
Who Lights Fires.

TABLE OF CONTENTS

The events of this story occur
a few hundred years before
The Legend of Black Jack.
It does not concern Jack Swift
or the folk tales that came to surround him.
This is the simple tale of one man
who discovered his Armor.

*T*hey say the Noble Seven came from the Waste.

They say they arrived from the desert gleaming in silvered mail, shimmering bright as the sun, a reflection of every color under God's sky. They were honor and righteousness and courage made flesh. Some say they came from beyond this sphere of existence, angels sent to stand against dæmons. Some say.

Many have called them Border Knights, though few realize how many borders they defended.

This is certain: they were beloved. Kings wanted to befriend them, queens wanted to marry them, and the poor folk wanted to become them. At one time, most children in Keymark could sing their colors.

Listen, my son, and learn every shade,
The Colors of Masters, the Knights of the Blade.
Come near me and sit you on one bended knee,
And I'll sing it to you as my dad sang it to me:
Amber for Dawning, Grace no man can earn;
Crimson for Midday, and Valor that burns;
Indigo for Dusk promised Truth of return.
Titian for Moon, and for Faith come what may;
Azure for Sky, and all Wisdom survey;
Jade for the Living, 'til Death pass away.
All rise up as One, united by Grey.
Listen, my daughter, and learn every shade,
The Colors of Masters, the Knights of the Blade.

They say the Border Knights were everything a man should be. Unsullied by the world, upright in virtue, immune to fear. They spent every waking moment in selfless service to Keymark, steely eyes fixed on the horizon, clad in armored glory like living statues. They were men of unshakeable faith, perfect in every way.

If you want to know the truth, I will tell you.

Chapter

1

WASTE

*"Is there any instinct more deeply implanted in
the heart of man than the pride of protection,
a protection which is constantly exerted for
a fragile and defenceless creature?"*

—Honoré de Balzac

S and screamed, threatening to rip flesh from bone.
No one had ever come this far into the Waste,
and with good reason. The last oasis had been three
hundred miles ago and all the men were dead or dying.

Howling winds ripped across the dunes at speeds that
would send a body flying. The surviving men stuck to the
slack between the towering dunes, travelling only at night,
when the winds were worst, to stay out of the deadly sun.
Tonight, just like last night, there was no food, no water,
no respite. They had trudged on foot ever since the last
camel died six days ago. They numbered twenty-two
pilgrims when they left Oruki, ten after Yosembi raiders
picked them off one by one. The fever took a few more.
Six days ago, the core group was separated in another
storm. Now they were only three men, each of them
weary, heat-sick, and nearly dead.

It was a rotten time for an ambush.

Gigantic insect legs burst from the sand all around
them, each a yard long, jointed at harsh angles, covered
in tan hair. Puce heads armed with huge mandibles
wriggled from the sand like dogs shaking off water.
Their inhuman shrieks pierced the air, deafening as the
howling wind.

Wenxu. Stahl reflexively reached for his shield,
which was three days gone, lost down a cliff face during
a Yosembi raid. *Damn.* Growling, he tried to rip his
stolen scimitar from its sheath, but the desert grit had
fused the scabbard's throat shut. *Yosembi junk!*

One of the monsters scuttled toward him on sharp legs. Stahl backed away, yanking at the pommel, trying to free his blade. *Come on, come on....* The insect lunged at him. Desperate, weaponless, he kicked the thing's head.

It didn't seem to notice.

The bug landed on him, legs crawling over his flesh, antennae flicking across his face.

"O for God's sake, come *on!*" Dying without a blade in his hand would be an embarrassment he would never live down. He spit on the throat of the scabbard and his gnarled hands finally tore the blade free with a squeal of metal.

"Ahh!" he shouted as the monster took him to the ground.

Claws raked at him. Teeth snapped at Stahl's eyes. Heart hammering against his chest, he backhanded the thing with his blade, severing a leg. A jet of putrid-smelling ichor spewed over his face.

"Yuk." he turned his head left, spitting. "Kid!"

The kid was surrounded by three big wenxu. He was putting up a good fight for a boy with a three-day fever, but those little pigstickers he carried weren't going to save him. Stahl heard a shout and turned to see his third companion, the soldier, being dragged away by more wenxu. *No choice. Get to the kid.*

Stahl's scimitar swung an arc that split his attacker in half. He regretted it instantly. Larval sacs gushed from its split belly, flooding over his arms, his legs, his

3

chest. They popped open. Little squiggly insects latched to him with sharp newborn legs. They bit at him, needle-mouths snapping, vomiting green slime. *Gross.* He squished one with a fist, eyes darting to the kid. *Now now now.*

He stood, covered in fifty pounds of writhing larvae, and strode forward.

The kid was in trouble. The three wenxu were piled on him, and Stahl couldn't tell the difference between the screams of the insects, the wind, or the boy.

Stahl lunged into to the pile of wenxu, grabbed one, and ripped off its head. Its body slumped to the ground, twitching. The other two wenxu kept going at the kid.

"Geddoff!" he yelled and snatched the mandible closest to the boy, tearing it away and hurling it into the wind.

The other wenxu pounced at him. *That's right, Sally, come get me.*

Stahl's boiled leather armor had survived ten years of hard use against monsters and men; the wenxu ripped it to shreds in ten heartbeats. Sally's mandibles slashed, tearing horrendous rends into his breastplate and kote. Stahl's eyes went wide and he screamed as her fangs bit down to the muscle. Larvae crawled up his neck, tearing at his face, going for his eyes. Sally leapt at him, latching on, clutching at him, riding him. Covered in screeching wenxu, he staggered under the onslaught.

Stahl almost fell, but if he lost his footing now, there would be no getting up again. *Protect the kid.* He dug in his heels and took the beating. Sally's cutting jaws came again. He threw up his left arm as she tore into him. Pain exploded as fangs struck bone.

But his right hand held the blade.

Stahl jammed it into the thing's neck, if Sally could be said to have a neck, and foul hemolymph exploded onto the sand. Shouting barbaric fury, he drove the curved steel into the wenxu over and over until the scimitar snapped in half.

Stahl kicked the body out of the way and took a painful step toward the kid, his little passengers still screeching in his ear. *Shut up, ugly babies.*

The last wenxu was on top of the boy, hacking away. The kid's eyes narrowed to slits as he buried one of his daggers down the wenxu's throat. A gauntlet of teeth shredded his arm, and he screamed. The thing made a choking sound, vomited yellow pus, and fell to the sand.

Stahl stomped on it, feeling the exoskeleton shatter under his boot. He extended a hand. "I told you, you need...*will you stop it?*" Stahl yelled at the larvae, smashing one that was trying desperately to eat his neck. "You need to graduate to swords."

"He's there!" The kid pointed through the sandstorm at a group of shadows, a soldier fighting monsters in the wind.

5

"Come on." Stahl dragged the boy to his feet.

The kid stared up at seven-foot Stahl Shian, his gigantic handlebar mustache, his shredded armor, his bleeding face, all covered in wriggling wenxu larvae. "Would you please kill those things?!"

"The meat goes bad ten minutes after they're dead," said Stahl. "I'm hungry. Now *move*." They ran for the soldier.

Sprinting through the wind, sand slashing his eyes, Stahl saw a wenxu corpse cut in half, legs still writhing. Another followed. The corpses formed a broken line that led to a pile of insect bodies. In the center of the pile, Stahl's last companion stood surrounded by five wenxu. They attacked as a tangled mass of spiny legs and the soldier went down.

Stahl outdistanced the kid, moving at a dead run. The wind picked up and the lashing sand masked his view of his friend being eaten alive. *Faster. Go faster.*

The wind gusted and he stumbled, blown nearly off his feet. Larvae were ripped from his body into the air, screaming as the wind took them. He heard the kid go down behind him. The wind rose to a yowl and, as if by majik, died suddenly. Sand whipped into a frenzy a thousand feet high began to fall from the sky like hissing rain.

Stahl saw the squirming insectile mass ahead. He watched three feet of steel flash through it like a farmer cutting wheat. Bodies dropped and splattered to the ground in a pile, leaking goo.

Stahl leapt amid the twitching corpses and grabbed the last remaining wenxu, a half-sized adolescent, by the throat, pulling it away to reveal the soldier. His eyes were closed, flat on his back. His armor was wrecked, broken pieces hanging by half-threads. Blond hair spilled over the sand, both smeared with his blood.

Stahl felt his heart rise into his throat. "Campion!"

Blue eyes opened. The soldier smiled, revealing perfect teeth.

Stahl breathed a sigh of relief. *Still alive.* He extended his free hand. "How do you still look good after *that?*"

"Good-looking parents." Campion Rei took his hand and rose. The blond soldier was caked in grit and bile, but he was still smiling, always smiling. He eyed the squirming wenxu lashing at Stahl's fist. "You keeping that one?"

"I'm thinking soup."

A crossbow bolt punctured the thing's head.

Stahl dropped the corpse and glanced toward the dune. On the steep slope, a wiry little figure cradled a crossbow on one narrow hip. A familiar silhouette. A friend.

"You look like crap," it said.

Abrahim. The old badger's still kicking.

Stahl managed a grin. "You're late. We already got 'em all."

"Been lookin' for you boys three days," came Abrahim's raspy voice. "You out here just farting around or what?"

Stahl smiled.

Another day above ground.

Still. It wouldn't have been a bad death.

"Kid's dead," croaked Abrahim.

Stahl turned. It wasn't true. The boy was just flat on his face, unconscious.

"I got him." Stahl jogged over and hiked the boy over his shoulder. He was heavier than he looked. *I forget he's still growing.*

The last of the flying sand from the storm settled and the harsh rasp of falling grit fell silent. Stahl looked up to find the sky clearing. He saw one moon against a black sky, then another.

Stahl's eyes twinkled, reflecting the orange and white of the moons, Gamilat and Anika. He the orange, she the white. He loved that story. *Gamilat always chasing, only joining with Anika for a time, before being torn apart again. Always. Forever.*

The two moons seemed even more beautiful in the desert sky. *Or maybe it's just a near-death thing.*

"So he's alive?" came Abrahim's voice.

"He's got a fever," said Stahl. "Pretty much since we split. How about you four?"

"Three." Abrahim had always been crusty, but now he sounded like he was talking through a throat full of sand. "He's still missing."

That's not good.

"Where are we headed?"

"South, two hours. Can you carry him?"

It wouldn't be the first time Stahl had carried one of his friends. "Sure."

Stahl looked up at the titian moon chasing the white and sighed, shifting the kid on his shoulders.

Lord Gamilat of the sky, always chasing, never catching, never completing his quest.

I'm beginning to understand how he feels.

———

"Stahl!" Farrior Han smiled as the group made their way into camp. He grabbed Stahl and pounded him on the back. "I was hoping you weren't dead!"

Farrior was a redheaded, round-shouldered six-footer who drew southpaw. He had a penchant for flowers and range weapons and was just odd enough that Stahl liked him best.

"Back atcha." Stahl grinned, relieved to see Farrior's face. He turned. "Hey Vyn." Resting against a lee, the hooded ranger raised one hand in greeting but said nothing. He looked green around the gills from fever.

Farrior slid his shoulder under the kid and took Stahl's burden in one smooth movement. He glanced at the big man. "You actually okay or just faking?"

Stahl cricked his back. "Yeah, I'm…whatever."

He was forty now, no spring chicken. He didn't bounce back the way he used to. His arm was going to take forever to heal. Still, he was breathing. That was worth something.

Farrior laid the kid down on a flat rock and went to work doing whatever things Farrior did in these situations. Farrior patched people. Stahl patched armor.

He unbuckled his useless breastplate and dropped it to the sand. *Dammit. Looks even worse than I thought.* He sighed. "Campion, let me see if I can do something with yours." The blond soldier unbuckled his gear and wordlessly dropped it at Stahl's feet. *Not much better. I might be able to strap some of that together. Maybe.* "Any water left?"

Farrior shook his head, tending to the kid. "All out. Even Abrahim. Got a baxbulb though. Last one." He offered the hairy bean-shaped pod. "Here."

"No."

"Take it."

Stahl wanted to. His mouth had been dry for days and his waterskin contained nothing but sand. He turned away, knowing the baxbulb would be too much temptation to resist. "Save it for the kid," he cleared his throat. "Your pauldrons are loose."

Stahl scooched over, re-laced the redhead's plundered Yosembi armor, and cinched it tight. He pulled out a strip of leather and went to work on Campion's gear.

Old patterns. Stahl the protector. Familiar as bread.

Farrior eyed Stahl's shredded leather armor. "Do I want to know what happened to yours?"

"Did its job."

"I don't think I've ever seen you without armor." Farrior tilted his head. "You look *weird*."

"You always look weird."

They should have shared a laugh then. Farrior had a great laugh, a goose-honk laugh. But they were too tired. The pair settled for dusty grins and a shared nod.

"Where's the captain?"

Farrior shook his head. "Had that look in his eye. Headed off on his own."

"To where?"

"Off."

Stahl sighed. "It's the voices again, isn't it?"

Farrior didn't say anything.

Once he finished working on the kid, he offered Stahl the remaining bit of beetleback, and they shared what passed for a meal out here in the Waste. That was the last of the food. There would be no more.

"Sun's coming up soon," Stahl murmured, pulling out his little mirror. He checked his mustache and frowned. The face in the looking glass was that of a monster. He was slashed by wenxu cuts, his lips were white and cracked, his skin was burned, and tan pustules were beginning to form on his neck from the xi bites. His face looked haggard and empty, ravaged by their time in the desert. He put the ugly reflection away. "We're going to have to button up for the sun."

"Do you still believe him?" came Farrior's voice.

"Yes."

Farrior squinted at the brightening horizon. "Believe him, or believe *in* him?"

"Is there a difference?"

"Forty days, Stahl. It's been forty days in the Waste." There was a grousing tone, a creeping crawl of uncertainty in his best friend's voice that Stahl didn't like. "And we're no closer now than we ever were. We're wandering around like dying beggars."

"Yeah."

"Have they spoken to you?"

Stahl snorted, but said nothing.

"They haven't talked to *me*. I don't know if they're real."

Stahl swallowed sand. "He says they're real."

"So where are they?" There was no answer. Just as there had been no answer last month, or the month before that, back in Oruki, when the captain first told them about the voices. "How are you holding out faith in him?"

"If he's wrong, we came out here to die." Stahl swallowed. "Better to hope he's right."

~⊹~

Stahl never slept well without his armor.

I don't need it, he tried to convince himself. *It's good to have but I don't need it.*

The hippopotamus in Oruki killed eleven people before the village asked for Stahl's help. He dispatched the beast and built his armor from its hide. Stahl had sewn his leathers stitch by stitch, feeling the soft peach fuzz as he worked, surprised by how supple it was. That flaw was corrected when he boiled it, using *cuir bouilli* to render greaves, vambraces, noida, cuisse, breastplate, and gauntlets tough as oak.

Gone now.

Ever since the incident when he was a kid, Stahl slept in whatever armor he owned. At first, it was just his shoes. Then leathers. Then, during the war, a breastplate and shield. Now, tonight, for the first time in a long time, nothing separated him from the world.

He rolled over in his blanket, rubbing his boots together. Stahl hadn't had naked feet since he was seven years old, awake or asleep. No point needing to flee and not being able to do it well.

He stared at the remains of his hippopotamus leathers. The noida plates might survive one more strike, but there was nothing to lash them to. The other pieces were ruined. He had lost his longneedle weeks ago, and even if he hadn't, there was too much structural damage for gut to repair.

He felt naked without armor. Vulnerable.

The helmet was still in his pack, as always. He hated the damn thing. Twenty hours crafting that leather bucket into the world, and he hated it. *How can you tell trouble is coming if you can't see or hear?*

He shifted uncomfortably, staring at the horizon. Sun was coming.

Seven years old. Long time ago. Maybe armor would have helped Mom and Dad. Shoes hadn't helped them run. He remembered the smoke and the yelling. Mostly, he remembered the kitten that licked Dad's blood off the floor. Stahl tried to remember his dad's face. He had a beard. His eyes were… brown? *Probably brown. It was a long time ago.*

All he really remembered from that night were two truths. *One: nowhere is safe. Two: find help.*

Stahl Shian did not remember his father or his mother. But he did remember the man who had come to the aid a seven-year-old kid all those years ago.

Sunrise broke the horizon. A single blossom of light.

Stahl watched it rise, and in that moment, he could swear he saw something.

He lifted his head. Yes.

Far off in the iron-flat desert, something was blocking the path of the heat.

Slowly, the speck grew. A silhouette, far away. It rose with the sun, little by little. Small. Silent. Steady.

Stahl sat up. There was no water, so he did not drink. There was no food, so he did not eat. He licked his parched lips, staring.

The speck became a figure. Upright. Tall.

Stahl heard Farrior rise to one elbow.

The figure kept coming, its pace long and measured.

A low howl of wind passed over the ridge. Stahl took his eyes away from the silhouette to check on his companions. Campion and the kid were still down. Farrior and Vyn were awake, watching. Abrahim was already in position on a tall rock, crouched and gazing at the sun.

I didn't hear him move. Has he been there all night? Abrahim was still as stone until the moment he stood up.

Stahl rose. Farrior came with him. Vyn sat up, collecting his bastard sword. Soon, the shape against the sun became a man.

Tall. Broad. Steady. He wore a wrap that had once been white, but the hardships of the Waste had bled it of dye, a cloak of no particular color. The hood was up, defending against the sun.

Vyn roused Campion. The soldier stayed with the boy, sharp eyes watching the shadow close in.

Stahl heard the crunching of the man's feet on the sand. His stride was rhythmic, hypnotic. Each step the same as the one before it. A steady pattern that did not falter.

Then he was there. Among them. One of them.

He walked past Stahl, continued past Farrior, past Vyn, past Abrahim's rock. He came to where Campion sat, and the drumbeat of his steps stopped.

He knelt, running a hand over the boy's forehead, brushing aside his hair.

The man leaned down, looked into the kid's pale face, then picked the boy up and heaved him onto his broad shoulder. Rising, he turned, situating his burden.

Then his steps began again, the same cadence as before.

He walked through the group of men, footsteps falling in his own tracks. Out to the flat pan into the warming sun.

Stahl watched the man's colorless cloak ripple in the breeze and saw his steel-grey eyes. A dry and sandy voice came.

"Found something."

The man passed on.

Stahl collected his gear. The others did the same. As always, Abrahim was first to join the walking man, striding the same tracks. The others were close behind.

Stahl looked at his broken armor. He wanted to bring it with him. The shredded leather wouldn't do him a lick of good ever again, yet still he wanted it.

I don't need it.

I don't.

He turned, following the man out into the salt flats, his thin shirt flapping against his skin, the sun shining brighter, growing hotter. The single file of men moved into the hardpan sunrise, following the steps of the grey man, their captain, Valerian Tsai.

Stahl's hippo leather lay behind, sand creeping up around the edges, no match for the Waste that would consume it. The sun rose higher, and the burnished leather was lost to memory as the starving men moved like a line of ants into the desert and disappeared into the horizon.

Chapter

W**ATER**

"Nothing is softer or more flexible
than water, yet nothing can resist it."
—**Lao Tzu**

S tahl heard it before he saw it, and by then, they had all broken into a run.

They passed the grey man, hollering, cheering, running, and tumbling down the lee. More than a trickle, it was an actual *creek*.

They buried their faces in it, gulping down water.

Campion sat in it and lay flat, letting the water pool around him. Vyn took off his boots and soaked his feet. Stahl finally found a use for his helmet, filling it in the stream and dumping it over Farrior's head.

The men laughed for the first time in a tenday, exhaling joy.

This. Stahl looked around, watching them laugh and splash. *This is what it's supposed to be.*

His eye wandered to the top of the ridge where Valerian Tsai and Abrahim still stood, talking. The captain and the little man, side by side, an unlikely pair.

"Farrior," came Abrahim's crackling voice. "Take care of him." He jerked his chin at the kid.

Stahl joined his friend to help carry the boy down the dune.

"Aren't you getting a drink?" Farrior asked.

"It's enough to know it's there," came Abrahim's reply.

Tough old badger.

They dragged the kid to the creek and got him in. Farrior Han plucked the buds of three nearby plants and jammed them in the kid's mouth. His eyes opened almost immediately, and he gasped for air.

Confused, the kid blinked and looked at Stahl. He turned his head and the creek ran into his mouth.

Bantam Pham spat it out, choking, then let go a weak laugh.

He *would* laugh. Stahl had always liked the kid's laugh, loud and musical. Bantam coughed suddenly, barking phlegm, the sickness ripping at his lungs. Then he started laughing again.

It was contagious. All of them started laughing with Bantam, welcoming him back. He looked like a confused wet puppy.

Valerian and Abrahim stayed on the rise, separate from the group. They always did this. Everyone played to their strengths. *Campion will join Valerian in a few minutes. I'll work perimeter. Vyn will hunt for game. Farrior will make food, the kid will sing a funny song, and we'll all have a good laugh.*

None of those things happened.

Valerian walked down the hill, followed by the old badger. "You okay?"

Bantam alternated between laughing and coughing. "Yeh. Heh."

"All right then." Valerian smiled. "Are you ready to meet them?"

Bantam's face stopped doing whatever it was doing. He took a few breaths, unbelieving. "Wh—you're serious?"

Stahl took a step closer. Farrior stood up. Vyn didn't move.

"We crossed more than just the Waste," Valerian said. "You can feel it, can't you? The air is different. This is somewhere *new*." He smiled. "We'll follow the creek." Valerian scooped a handful of water and drank. He exhaled an *ah* of pleasure. "And we'll see."

He strode on, his feet splashing in the water as he went.

~ ⨯ ~

A second creek appeared as they traveled upstream, following the source. Soon enough, it turned into an actual stream, rippling through the gullies of the desert. They saw their first tree, then another. A fennec fox. Bird nests. Life.

Moving up the desert delta, the water gained momentum. The rock rose on either side and soon they were walking sandy stone trails above what had become a river.

Stahl took point, Campion right behind him. Old patterns. Everyone lined up like always. The seven of them could break an ambush four ways from this position, but Stahl wished for more protection. They were still too exposed.

The river had burrowed holes through the rock over the course of centuries, and little pools became common. Acacias, willows, and eucalyptus grew thick, scenting the air as bare rock gave way to lush jungle cliffs and waterfalls.

Stahl drank, water still a delightful novelty. After so long in the desert, it felt odd to not be able to see the horizon, and he was startled to turn a bend to find their path at an end. He took a step back. It was a stone cliff with trees growing out of it and a narrow crack near the top. There was nowhere to go but up.

He clambered up a tree root burrowed into the rock wall and peered through the thick leaves. The crack in the rock was open, a path forward. He gestured for the men to climb up.

Stahl made his way through the narrow passage in the stone, scouting ahead. Leaves sprouted everywhere. He moved through it all blindly. All he had to go on was sound—

A splash. Too big.

Something ahead. He held up his hand, forcing a halt. He could not see through the wall of leaves covering the gap in the rock, but he could hear the sound from where he stood. Movement.

More than one of them. Whatever they are.

There was no way to go but forward. Any flanking was impossible from here, the space was too narrow and too steep.

Stahl looked back.

Valerian nodded.

Wishing for a shield, Stahl pushed through the green curtain to the other side...

…and saw women bathing in natural pools beside a cascading waterfall.

His jaw fell.

Their laughter was like birdsong. They splashed each other, disappearing into one pool and resurfacing in another. A few lounged in the sun. One played a tune on a twin flute. A slim figure slid down one of the falls, gliding over the smooth rock into the pool. Another jumped from a high cliff, her body making a long arc in the air, her smile an invitation to joy, then *splash*.

Stahl blinked, dumbstruck.

The aroma of broiling butter stroked him like a lover's hand as he turned his eyes to their camp. A large and colorful tent stood draped in myriad shades of greens and blues. A long cookfire emitted a perfume of savory delights. Large clay pans were nestled over the fire and Stahl could smell asparagus, rosemary, garlic, mushrooms, herrykin, onions, cheeses, and baking bread. Slim male figures moved from one savory delight to the next, preparing supper.

Roasted butter.

Corn on the cob.

Stahl salivated.

The women in the pool washed themselves, singing:

Sister spinning on the leaf
Flicker candle O so brief
Arid form, so dusty dry
One dusky note of meadowlark
Surrenders she unto the dark
As she whispered ever now goodbye
Forever dry dry dry dry dry.
Dry dry dry dry dry.

Sister spinning dark prevail
Emerges softly nightingale.
He sings to her his waking lullabye
Silence crouches on her chest
Forever drifting dispossessed
Heart beating out the blood so mystified
Forever dry dry dry dry dry.
Dry dry dry dry dry.

Sister spinning tell me true
Were you for he and he for you
Water flowing gently as she dies
Green pools of water full immersed
But naught can slake her aching thirst
Come nightingale and sing upon her thigh
O never dry dry dry dry dry.

"What do you see?" came Campion's whisper from the distance.

"Go away." Stahl's eyes never left the women. *They aren't sylphs. Or naiads. They're something better.*

"Stahl."

Just one more minute. Just one more.

"Stahl." Campion came through the branches and stopped cold, staring.

One of the fey women rose from the water and walked elegantly across the rock, squeezing the water from perfect hair. *Dry dry dry dry dry.*

"O Lord and Lady, what are those?" came Campion's hushed voice.

"Women." Stahl blinked. "You've seen one before, right?"

"They're not jaelin. They're just—they're the most beautiful—"

Stahl smiled. "You've found your match, Campion. They're prettier than you."

Campion nodded, speechless.

"What do you see?" came Bantam's voice.

"Go away," they both said together.

But the majik had fled. Bantam, Abrahim, and the others were coming. Stahl took one last look at unbroken perfection and sighed.

Okay. Time to break it.

Stahl walked into the clearing and cleared his throat. "*Ahem.* Excuse me, ladies."

Their heads turned to him and each lovely face broke into a smile. They rose from the pools as one, gathering on rocks and outcroppings to gaze upon the interloper.

Stahl stepped forward. "I was wondering if—um, I was just passing and heard your song and saw you swimming—you are very good swimmers by the, very…athletic. I swim a bit myself, I'm from a fishing village—I mean, hello—"

He felt a hand on his shoulder. Abrahim. The little man squinted at him. "You're not good at talking to people, Stahl. Let him do it."

Stahl turned to find Valerian Tsai standing behind him. Stahl stepped back and allowed the captain to take center stage.

Thank God.

Valerian's eyes gleamed.

Seven years, thought Stahl. *Seven years he has been waiting for this moment.*

Seven years from the night Valerian Tsai had first heard the voices, from the time they had first whispered to him, whispered what was needed. Seven years from the moment he first began to believe. To plan. Picking his men from the war in Oruki. Assembling the caravan. Achieving what no man ever had, just to get to this place right now.

"I am Valerian Tsai." His voice was strong. "You quested me, and I have come."

One statuesque figure, the tallest and by far the most beautiful, stepped forward from the camp. Her hair was free to her waist, black as a raven. Her eyes were silver and indigo, dancing in a mysterious light. A long, tight-fitting wrap of what appeared to be sapphires and flowing water clung to her curves, accentuating every inch of her figure. She smiled and spoke.

"I am Twilight of the Elder," her voice came rich as honey, rumbling with power. "I quested you, and you have come, paladin."

Valerian Tsai strode forward and presented his dirty, cracked, sand-ravaged hand palm-up.

She took it gracefully, slender fingers reaching for him. He bowed and kissed her hand. As he rose, she placed one hand on his shoulder and leaned in, pressing her forehead to his. Both closed their eyes as a silent moment passed between them.

"That is the most beautiful woman I have ever seen in my life," murmured Bantam. "They're angels, right? We're dead?"

None of them responded. None of them knew.

Valerian and the woman finally broke their reverie.

"These are my men," said Valerian, gesturing for the fellowship to come closer. "Abrahim Qin, my thoughts. Campion Rei, my arm." Both men stepped forward and bowed. "These are Stahl, Farrior, Vyn, and Bantam, my bone, my blood, my heart, and my hope. They are the best of men."

Stahl blushed. He made every attempt to meet the fey woman's eyes, but in the end, he was forced to avert his gaze. She was too beautiful to look at.

There was no armor against that face.

"I am grateful to you all." Her voice was quiet music. "Your trials have been on our behalf. We honor your sacrifice. Welcome, brethren. Let us refill your cup."

She gestured for them to follow.

Farrior glanced at Stahl, his eyes dancing. "Is this real?"

I don't know but I hope so.

Fey women came forward. They bowed to the seven men. Stahl was briefly struck with the scene: a bevy of the most beautiful creatures in the world bowing before a passel of filthy, ragged vagabonds clad in rags and grit.

Stahl stared at his boots.

One of the women came to him and began removing his cloak. He stiffened, embarrassed. He felt sorry for her, having to smell the stink and sweat of seven hundred miles, suddenly ashamed as her pale, perfect fingers touched the dried blood of his garments. "No, wait—"

"Please." She looked up at him. "I am Bharal." Her white hair drifted over frost-blue eyes, her skin so healthy it glowed. "You honor us by your presence Stahl Shian. Allow me to fill your cup."

He gave up resisting and decided to just fall in love with her.

Maybe this is a dream, and we are all enchanted. Maybe they kill us all now, or quietly in our sleep. Still.

It would not be a bad death.

Lounging in the water, Stahl ate another ear of corn as Bharal washed his hair. Butter dripped down his chin. There was some kind of spice on the corn—*paprika?*—that made him close his eyes as he savored every bite.

He had given up trying to impress the fey women or trying to be dignified. After the first bite, he had eaten like a *yaban hito*, devouring the roasted vegetables, sumptuous fruits, sweet cream, savory butter, and crispy breads with a vigor he didn't know he possessed. The women took it in good humor. They were beautiful, yes, but Stahl was more impressed with their aura of radiant strength, the power of the *wikk* they all wore like a coat of armor.

"I think I'm happier than I have ever been," Farrior said, popping a fat, pink berry into his mouth. Chevrotain, a dark-skinned woman with powerful arms and amber irises, had appointed herself his attendant. She scrubbed the sand from Farrior's broad shoulders with pale linen. "Right. This. Second."

Stahl closed his eyes as Bharal worked her fingers through his hair, building a lather. "Thank you, Bharal," he said as one of her handmaids handed him a fourth ear of corn. "Can I live here? Will you be my wife?"

She smiled, her eyes twinkling. "You are very funny, Stahl Shian. Someday you will find one far more suited to your tastes than I."

"Bharal, I've never even *imagined* a woman as perfect as you." She laughed like flowing water.

"Ladies, would you be willing to get us another round of that pineapple?" asked Farrior. "And that crispy naan, if you please."

Bharal and Chevrotain nodded and made for the camp. They passed the bonfire where Vyn stripped off the last of his Waste clothes and threw them in, letting them burn. Vyn followed a fey into the pool where Campion, Abrahim, and Bantam were already being scrubbed to a cleanliness they had not known for months.

"So," Farrior sighed. "What happens now?"

Stahl leaned his head back and closed his eyes. "Pineapple."

"No, genius. With *them*." Farrior pointed.

Valerian's black hair gleamed with moisture as he huddled in conversation with the tall woman near the fire. He wore new homespun linen, but he still would not give up that cloak. It lay folded neatly by his side, a memento of their trials. *Sentimental, our captain.*

"I dunno." Stahl munched on a hunk of iced mango. "Something."

"Who *are* these people?"

"And how do they have actual *ice?*"

"Are they tennin?" Farrior squinted, as if that would help. "Or maybe kalpit baune?"

"Maybe Bantam's right. Maybe they're angels." Stahl cocked his head, chewing. "What kind of a name is Twilight?"

"You want to call her Twila and see what happens?"

"No." Stahl glanced at the woman. She was different from the rest of these people. Bigger. More powerful.

31

Even the strong men who worked the camp looked frail in her presence. She radiated power, wreathed in a majik more powerful than steel. "No I do not."

Farrior looked up at the waterfalls, the trees, the camp. "This isn't their home." He scratched at his newly trimmed red beard. "Too much gear. They came out here to wait for us."

"Uh-huh," said Stahl.

"What do you think they're saying to each other?"

"Uh-huh."

Farrior chuckled. "You don't care at all, do you?"

"I care about this corn."

"This isn't some fishing village in Oruki. I don't even know if we're in the same *sphere* anymore, Stahl. I mean, look at them. Something big is going on here."

"That's for *him* to figure out." Stahl gestured with his corncob at the captain. "It's his vision. His call. Whatever he decides, I'll do." He took another bite. "I'm satisfied."

He had followed the captain without question for years. They all had. Two wars, a dozen campaigns, and the trip across the Waste *(and what more?)* had cemented Stahl's faith. He was protected from the agony of indecision. Where Valerian went, he went.

"Stahl."

"Yeah?"

"Are you still wearing shoes?"

He had hoped they wouldn't notice when he stripped down beneath the water. Hoped they wouldn't see that his feet were still encased in leather.

I still might need to run.

"I took the boots off, didn't I?"

"You wear shoes in your *boots?*"

Stahl shrugged. "The bottoms of your feet are the most vulnerable spot on your body, Farrior. Worst design I've ever seen. One injury and you're immobile. If you don't have shoes, you're useless. Feet." He spat. "We should have paws or hooves." Farrior snorted a laugh. Stahl pointed at him. "You ever try to run barefoot? Over rock? You won't get far."

"Stahl." Farrior leaned in. "What if we don't *have* to run?" He spread his hands, gesturing to the paradise around them. "What if we're safe?"

"No such thing."

Farrior shook his head. "You're addicted to armor, Stahl."

The big man watched Bharal and the mysterious fey returning, bearing more fruit. "Maybe."

Farrior shrugged, giving up. "So. If this isn't where they live, what do you think their home looks like?"

"I don't know," said Stahl, eyeing the approaching women. "But I bet it's spectacular."

~

White volcanoes thundered in the distance. Red cracks in the lava spewed glowing-hot magma that rose and fell back to the mountain's maw—a never-ending ring of vomitus fire.

Stahl leaned on one knee and exhaled a low whistle.

"Now, that's a thing I've never seen."

They were on a rise, looking out over the strange valley below. The seven men stood, the fey and Twilight behind them. The men stared, trying to take it all in. A ring of white volcanoes twenty miles wide encircled a thick, emerald forest so lush it seemed its own private world of living green nestled within the steaming bosom of molten fire.

"How are they white?" asked Bantam.

Campion turned. "What?"

"How are the volcanoes white?" The kid pointed. "The lava goes down the side, it cools, it should turn black."

"Seen a lot of mountains breathing fire, have you?" scowled Abrahim.

"But why does it turn white?"

"I dunno, maybe they paint it," said Stahl. "The real question is why does it look like the only defense they built"—he pointed—"is *that?*"

An incomplete white wall lay in pieces between the largest gap in the volcanoes.

Oxen dragged heavy loads, hauling half a quarry's worth of stone closer to its final position at the solitary wall. Tall fey men called out commands from the tops of rubble. At the apex of the huge circular barrier, where a great door would stand, two curving pillars rose, drawing toward each other at the peak like Gamilat and Anika, not quite touching.

"Look at the line of it," whistled Farrior. "How did they make a perfect circle?"

Stahl had no eye for architecture, but even he could tell the finished result would be magnificent.

Stunning really.

But useless.

"*Semi*-circle. It doesn't touch anything on either side."

Farrior ignored him, shaking his head. "I mean it's perfect."

"All you have to do is go around it," said Stahl, pointing. "It's indefensible."

"I..." Farrior stalled. "Wait, what? It's..." Farrior blinked, suddenly baffled. "Why *wouldn't* an enemy just go around it?"

"And where's the castle?" asked Stahl, flicking a finger at it. "They put up a big wall to protect...what? Nothing?"

Bantam bit into an apple. "Maybe it's decorative."

That thing has got to be the worst defense I've ever seen.

As they drew closer, an ox team finished hauling a heavy load of albino rock to its destination. The curtain wall was so short Stahl could see over it.

Useless.

The stone on the cart was cut at perfect right angles that looked sharp enough to make a man bleed. The white was perfect, spotless. It didn't seem like any masonry work Stahl had ever seen; it looked like it had been minted whole from someone's imagination.

As Stahl watched, one of the huge stones in the cart lifted a few inches into the air.

He stopped, staring.

The stone rose upward unsupported.

It moved through the air slowly, turning as it came toward the wall, then found its place in the world, cut exactly to the wall's dimensions. Stahl heard the light rumble as rock whispered against rock and the piece landed home. There was no seamline he could see; the piece had become part of a larger whole.

As another stone slowly lifted from the cart, Stahl saw the fey men standing with their eyes closed, murmuring softly. As their pitch rose, so did the stone, and the fey were lost from view behind it.

Well, I'll be damned.

"Wizards!" said the kid, grinning like an idiot.

Campion frowned. "If they're wizards, why do they need us?"

As they moved along the curtain wall, Twilight and her retinue paused at the first tower, a rounded outcropping.

Twilight glided forward and took Abrahim's hand.

He allowed her to take it with more grace than Stahl would have given the old man credit for. She walked backward, smiling, leading him.

As they approached the tower base, Stahl saw there was a ten-foot niche cut into the wall, ornamented with scrollwork and filigree, more beautiful than the rest. Within the alcove was a short stone plinth.

Upon the pedestal was a statue wearing the finest steel Stahl Shian had ever seen.

Rapturous joy swelled in his heart the moment he laid eyes on it. *Perfect.* A full complement of plate mail adorned the stone figure. Embossed in scintillating opal, the steel itself was sky-blue and gleamed with pearlescent luster fresh from the forge. It fit tight against the statue with not an inch of space between stone and metal. Banded rings of azure steel coursed around the statue's body like water, elegant and perfect and complete.

The statue itself was a perfect replica of Abrahim Qin.

The likeness was uncanny. His broken nose, his bald head, his sharp jaw and sharper cheekbones, all replicated perfectly by the hands of a master artisan. The figure struck a heroic pose, one arm raised, mouth shouting orders, one eyebrow cocked into the angry curl all of them knew so well.

Still holding the true Abrahim's hand, Twilight fell to one knee and bowed. The fey women followed her movement, bending their knees before him. The area behind the wall fell silent, and Stahl knew the men inside were bowing too.

There was a gleam in Abrahim's eye. His weathered face broke into a rare smile. His chest filled. He bent forward and delicately kissed the lady's hand. His lips pressed against her skin for a long moment, then he bid her rise.

She kissed him on one cheek, then the other. After a breath, she bowed again, then stepped toward Campion. She extended her hand, and he took it.

In that manner they moved along the curtain wall. Each statue was more glorious than the next. Campion's handsome face, Vyn's high cheekbones, Farrior's easy grace; all of them were almost more real than the men themselves. *But the armor....*

Every other suit of plate, chain or splint Stahl had seen in his entire life was armor. This was Armor.

Each suit was perfectly crafted for each man's fighting style. Abrahim's was made of a hundred interlocking pieces, allowing him maneuverability, his true strength. Bantam's cuisses, poleyns, and greaves were smaller, granting him the speed he used so well. Campion's breastplate was peaked in the center and atop the helm to turn away blows from multiple opponents, built for a man who dove into the thickest part of the fight. Vyn's pauldrons and couters were ridged, an advantage for a man who liked to throw his body around. Farrior's was heavy on the right side, spare on the left, built for a southpaw. Each in his own color. Vyn's ranger green, Farrior's sunny yellow, Campion's bloody red.

Twilight reached for Stahl.

He swallowed once and allowed himself to take her delicate hand.

He desperately wanted to look ahead, to see his double and the Armor that adorned it. But all he could see were her eyes. He had looked into deep pools before, but not like this. He felt her adoration, her pride pulling gently at the deepest part of his soul. He heard her voice in his mind, a tickling whisper of *thank you, thank you, thank you.*

She was magnificent.

And she bowed before him.

A silence fell over him. There was a moment where nothing moved, nothing mattered but him. Even his friends were silent with reverence. Stahl breathed in deep. He kissed her hand and looked up.

He felt his heart catch in his throat.

Rondels. They used rondels.

Double-thick disc plates bolstered the shoulders, the chest, the gauntlets. Armor upon armor. The left vambrace was thick as a stovepipe, as much a shield as he would ever need. Besagues protected the underside of his arms. True sabatons for his feet. But most dear to his heart was the color. Veins of aventurine quartz radiated out from each rondel in concentric circles—an identical orange to Gamilat, the warming moon.

Atop the finest armor he had ever seen in his life or imagined in his dreams was his own face. His hawk nose, his bushy eyebrows, his heavy handlebar mustache. Even his left earlobe was missing. His long arms, thick thighs, and broad shoulders were leaning forward in a defensive stance, left arm up. Stahl could almost see the child behind him, the one he was protecting.

He looked like a hero.

Stahl had no idea how long he stared at the statue. It could have been a century for all he knew. His life changed in that century. He knew exactly who he wanted to become.

When his eyes broke with his mirror, Stahl turned to find six true men waiting to join him.

~+~

Valerian Tsai's Armor stood central to the fountain within the bailey. It showed no face, the helmet completing the perfect image of a radiant knight.

Valerian did not inspect it, nor did the lady bow to him. Valerian simply turned and called for a circular table, which was produced straightaway by the fey.

Chairs quickly followed, and Stahl was seated. The table was swiftly covered in white velvet, and water goblets and several plates of fruit appeared. Stahl looked around at his brothers.

After witnessing their statues, Stahl viewed his friends differently now.

They all seem... better.

Even Farrior. The man felt like a fountain of goodness, the hero in the statue, not the scraggly brawler Stahl traded insults with. Not the guy who burned breakfast twice a month and farted in his sleep.

Stahl slapped his knees, calling everyone's attention. "All right, Valerian," he said sharply. "Maybe these dream-people of yours actually exist after all."

Abrahim laughed. Bantam snorted, then giggled. All of them chuckled.

Valerian smiled at Stahl, then rapped his knuckles on the table. "So. Thank you for following me here. Thank you for believing in me, even when your lives were at risk. You're good men. And these people"—he gestured to the men and women who stood in a wide ring around the table at a respectful distance—"need your help."

"And who exactly *are* these people?" asked Campion.

"They are called elves."

The men glanced at each other, puzzled looks on their faces. *Sylphs, fey, naiads, dryads, faeries, yōkai, tennin*…those they knew. Stahl looked at Valerian, mouthing the unfamiliar word. "Elves? What's an *elve?*"

"Elf." Valerian smiled. "Elves are a people, and they created this place."

Bantam looked around. "This wall?"

"This world."

The men shifted in their seats. Valerian nodded. "This land upon which we stand, the water we drink,

41

the very air we breathe, they created it all. Everything since the Waste. This place is called Keymark, and the elves made it from nothing but ash."

Bantam blinked. "So are they wizards or gods?"

"They are makers." Valerian leaned forward. "They are making this land as we speak. They are growing the volcanoes to make a ring around their home, their forest, the Elder Wood"—he gestured toward the vast forest behind him—"to protect it. But the volcanoes are still too small, and the wall is incomplete. It will not be ready in time."

"In time for what?"

"The attack."

Campion leaned back. Abrahim nodded. Bantam opened his mouth, raising a finger.

"Before you ask"—Valerian raised his hand—"I don't know how many are attacking. More than us. Bigger than us. And sometime in the next day."

Farrior eyed Stahl. Vyn scowled and leaned in. "Reinforcements?"

"It's just us."

A surprised murmur from the men.

"What about them?" The kid jerked his chin at the elven architects. "They aren't going to defend themselves?"

"They will not kill," Valerian said. "They are makers. They cannot destroy. And they have spent seven years"—he looked around the table —"summoning seven men to protect them."

"Ridiculous," Campion barked. "They're under attack. It's kill or be killed."

Abrahim eyed him. "It's not ridiculous," he said sharply. "It's honorable. And impractical."

"It doesn't matter either way." Stahl put his feet up on the table and crossed his arms. "This whole setup is a boondoggle." Everyone looked at him. No one knew defense like Stahl. "These bigger-than-us folk will just flank us through the woods. There's nothing to defend and no way to defend it."

Valerian shook his head. "Our hosts claim they can hold the forest. They can mislead them with their majik. For a while. The only safe passage into the Elder Wood is there."

The captain pointed behind him to a rock mound with a small cave just big enough for a horse. At the end of the short passage was a simple wooden gate, half-open, silhouetted by the warm golden-green light of the trees beyond. The entire arch wall was curved around that single entrance into the forest.

Doubtful looks passed between the men. "Assume that's true." Stahl shrugged. "We might be able to funnel an attack, but we need that arch completed *right now*. There's a big hole in the center of the wall. We need a big door to cover it."

Valerian shook his head. "No door."

Campion slammed a hand on the table and cursed. The men reacted, leaning back. Even Abrahim raised an eyebrow. It was a rare outburst from the captain's right hand.

Valerian stared at Campion; his iron eyes shone. "The job is to defend this border," he said, leaning over the table. "And to keep it open."

"Open for who?" asked Bantam, curious as always.

"Open for those who seek the elves without meaning them harm," said Valerian. "People like us."

"Open," said Campion. "Defend against an attack with an open door?" He snorted. "It's impossible."

"Open," growled Abrahim, scowling.

Open. Stahl blinked. *They want us to do it without defenses.*

Two men tried to talk at the same time, then four. It was a cacophony of arguments and thoughts, fallen to incoherent babble.

Dammit. It didn't happen often, and it was never pretty, but the argument would flare out in a few minutes. It always did. *What they need is a joke*, thought Stahl. *What's a good you're-all-going-to-die joke?*

Campion said, "I'm not going to fight with one hand tied behind my back just so these people—"

Stahl kicked the table with a bang. The men flinched, and glared at him.

He pointed at the captain.

"They have taken an oath not to kill," said Valerian Tsai, his voice steady. "Their paladins are to defend them from those who mean them harm. And their paladins will keep the way open to those who do not.

"In return they offer this wall, this ward and everything in it as home, to do with as we please, live in as we like, and call our own. They offer food and drink and shelter and comfort as long as we choose to stay, as well as a knight's oath and title. They offer us the Armor." He took a deep breath. "And they offer these."

The elves lay silver swords upon the round table, points in, unique to each man. Ideal for armor without a shield, the hand-and-a-half steel gleamed bright majik. Stahl watched Gamilat's titian moonlight, the same shade as his Armor, dance within the crossbar of his offered blade.

"You have believed in me since I first told you of my visions. Let me tell you what I believe," said Valerian, standing straight. "I believe it is divine providence we are seven men serving our seventh siege in our seventh year. I believe we are ordained to be here and stand this ground. I believe our lives have shaped us like the earth shapes a diamond, and our lives have made us, the seven of us, strong enough to withstand anything. I believe we were made for this place. You've followed me this far on faith. I ask you to follow me one step further."

Six warriors stared at him, unblinking. The captain was not stingy with his praise, but he had never said anything like that before. Stahl sat a little straighter.

"Know this: I will not stay here without you," said Valerian. "If even one of you thinks this is not the right choice, that acting as defenders of the elves is not what you want, I will go into the sands with you and return to Oruki. It is all of us, or none of us."

A long breath. The wind stilled.

Abrahim Qin stood. He offered a sharp nod. Farrior and Stahl rose together. Bantam followed them, leaping to his feet. Vyn was last.

Only Campion remained seated. His right hand fingered the hilt of the crimson knight's blade before him. The wind picked up and tousled his golden hair. Blue eyes scanned each one of them, landing on Valerian.

"Would you keep your word?" he asked quietly, looking at the black-haired captain. "Would you go back to the Waste today? Would you give this up?" He gestured around them at the wall, the table, the elven supplicants. "Would you give up *that?*" He pointed at the Armor behind Valerian, gleaming on its pedestal. "Would you really give it up if I said no?"

"I will." There was no hesitation in Valerian's reply. "Say the word and we will cross the Waste and be friends forevermore."

Campion clicked his tongue. "I really believe you would." He slapped his hands on his knees. "Well…" He stood. "I'm not making my mind up until I see what I'm defending." He left the table and walked past the silver statue, heading toward the cave.

The rest of the men watched him go, then glanced at each other and followed.

Farrior trotted up beside Stahl. "Do you think he's going to say no?"

"Who knows? It's Campion."

"Are you sure we're doing the right thing? This is a big leap."

Vyn caught up to them. "Stahl. Can we win here?"

"I…" Stahl looked back at the wall. "I don't know."

Bantam jogged to catch up. "What are you talking about?"

"Whether we're in or not."

"Wait, I thought…" the kid stammered. "When Abrahim stood up, I thought we were *all* supposed to stand up. Are you guys not in?"

None of them answered.

None of them knew.

At the back of the short cave was a little wooden gate with no lock, hanging open. As Stahl passed through, he was surprised to see how green the forest was from inside, how thick the canopy. Enormous trees stretched tall over a carpet of moss and earth and water.

Somehow, there was sunlight. Beneath the trees, the sun shimmered, forming long rays of light dancing across flora and fauna alike.

Gorgeous.

The air was thick and humid one moment, then refreshed by a breeze the next. Little firelights danced in the air, wafting in the soft wind.

Stahl closed his eyes and breathed deeply. He felt good, as if all his burdens had been erased by majik. Something *better* than majik.

His shoulders loosened; the lines of his face smoothed. His eyes opened, letting the sensation of the elven green wash over him like the sea.

One of the fireflies danced nearby, and Stahl glimpsed a tiny pair of pale female legs dangling beneath glowing dragonfly wings. It tittered and sped away. He couldn't help but smile.

The seven men walked on into the forest, exploring. There was something about the Elder Wood that was impossible to define, something… liberating. The longer they stayed, the more their spirits lifted. Vyn began laughing. Bantam suddenly let out a whoop and started running. Farrior hooted in delight and took off after him like children playing in the forest. Finally, the scowl broke from Campion's face as he raced after them, laughing.

Walking through the forest light, Stahl felt free. There was peace all around him. For the first time in memory, he didn't have the haunting feeling that something might attack him right this second.

It was unnerving.

Nobody can get me. Not now.

Lagging behind the others, Stahl looked at the forest floor. Verdant moss covered everything, a woven carpet of spongy green. He knelt and peeled off his gauntlet, feeling the surface, soft and pliant.

He looked around, noticing his companions were farther away now. He glanced to each side, making sure no one could see him, then hunkered down in the bushes.

It wouldn't be a bad death.

He took a deep breath, then removed one of his shoes.

He looked at his naked foot a moment. It had been a long time since he had seen those toes. Carefully, he pressed them into the ground. Soft moss nuzzled the exposed skin of his foot. It tickled and he jerked away. He shuddered, then allowed his toes to touch down again. He almost laughed but stopped himself.

Stahl looked around again, checking to see if the coast was clear.

Rising, he removed his remaining shoe and placed his other bare foot on the forest mat. Something unlocked in his chest as he looked down and saw ten helpless pink piggies nestled in the green moss.

Then, finally, he let himself laugh.

3

WALL

*A thorn defends the rose,
harming only those who would
steal the blossom.*
—Chinese Proverb

The sound of armor-buckles rattled along the outside of the wall as seven men suited up.

Stahl knew the elven aegis was well-made, but he had not realized how well. It bolted perfectly into place. The plates, twenty-one of them, fused into position the moment the buckles snapped. Stahl's layered clothes flattened against his flesh. *Tight tight tight.*

He *klonged* his metal shoes against the wall, checking for waggle. *Nope.* He buckled the thigh armor, then the fauld, cullet, and codpiece. *Ow. Too tight.* Inhaling, Stahl bolted the kote and do, locking up his lean midsection. The breastplate was tightest of all. He had to strain to buckle it. When it clamped shut, he was surprised he could draw breath, but it seemed to flex with him. Rerebraces, vambraces, the coulter and, finally, all seven magnificent rondels.

Last was the helmet. Stahl frowned. He hated being inside a helmet, any helmet. It made him claustrophobic.

Bad peripherals, slow movement, lousy hearing. It's like trying to fight underwater. He glared at the metal in his hands. *Why did you even give me a helmet? You're all such whoop-de-doo know-it-alls, why didn't you soothsay that I won't wear one?*

Might as well get it over with.

Stahl buckled on the bucket.

He rattled his head back and forth, felt it tighten against his skull. He cricked his neck and shot out a breath, opening his eyes.

There was no helmet. He looked left, he looked right. He could feel it, but the thing simply refused to block his vision. Left again. *No.* Right. *No.* He bashed his fist into the side of his helmet, trying to clear his head. Nothing. *I can't see my helmet.* What's more, he could feel the wind as well.

I've worn hats that were worse than this.

Stahl grinned. "Hey guys! Put on your helmets! Farrior! Put on the *helm!*"

Everybody looked so good. Farrior shone, his golden blandishments gleaming in the light, creating their own illumination. The redhead turned and broke into a grin. "Hey, we're matchers!" It was true. His color was closest to Stahl's, a bright yellow to his darker orange, and each made the other look warmer and more vibrant.

"Ha," said Stahl. "They knew to put us together."

Vyn looked fantastic in gleaming emerald threads of majik. Campion looked splendid, no surprise there, tall and bullfighter red. Bantam looked like a preening purple peacock. Even Abrahim looked like five feet of blue sex. *Never thought I'd think that.*

Stahl looked around. "Anybody need help?" No one took up his offer. All seven men were buttoned up tight.

"It's light," said Abrahim, bouncing. He dropped to a roll and went left, springing back up on one foot. He moved easily as if wearing a loincloth. "Ha. *Very* light." He twisted, stretching, feeling the steel move with him.

"Come on." Bantam ran ahead through the unfinished arch.

Twilight waited with six women at the central fountain, each holding a sword pressed to their breast. Valerian was already there, dressed in his silver Armor, helm off. He smiled as they approached. His voice was brimming with pride. "You are magnificent."

They laughed and made similar responses regarding his Armor. Every suit was perfect, but Valerian's was the pinnacle, shining brightest. *It suits him.*

Campion lifted the visor on his helm. "The Silver Knight."

"Silver is too far above me," said Valerian. "Grey will do."

"Hey," said Farrior, trying to mimic Campion's movement. "Why doesn't my visor come up?"

"Huh," murmured Abrahim. "Neither does mine."

"Mine does." Bantam waggled his up and down.

Stahl shrugged. "I don't even have one."

"Because all three of you are ugly." Campion smiled. "The elves *are* wise."

That got a laugh. Farrior gave him a kick as they stood in a line and then knelt together.

Valerian Tsai drew his sword, standing before them. He incanted the words that would bind them to this place and to each other.

Valerian spoke and the men repeated.

I swear by my faith and the men beside me, I will defend this stone, this water, and this wood. I will protect the elves from those who would do them harm. By my faith, I will stand to keep this border open to the weak, to the needy, to those seeking solace, and never to bar their passing. I stand as paladin to the Elder Wood, a light against the dark. Let it be so.

Stahl accepted his titian blade from the elven woman. Gamilat's light, always chasing but never catching, thrummed up his arm, powerful.

They stood as one, swords raised.

Valerian spoke, "From this day to our last. Brothers."

"Brothers."

Seven swords came together and rang as one bell.

Stahl rubbed at his neck. "Are your clothes itching?"

The new knights stood outside the wall, watching the stone edifice rise bit by bit. The approach on the elven arch was the simplest one of all: flat grasslands. No tricks, no sneak attacks. The only thing an enemy could do here was to come straight at you.

Now all we have to do is figure how to stop them. Whoever they are.

Stahl rubbed at his neck. "Are your clothes itching?"

"Itching?" Farrior blinked at him.

Stahl reached down his gorget, pulling at the cloth. "Mine's all bunched up. Hang on." He unbuckled his breastplate.

"We stand together in the middle at the arch," said Campion. "The enemy must come there. If they're looking for a fight, we *are* the fight."

"Not if they're smart," grumbled Abrahim. "I've seen plenty of battles, Campion. They'll spread us out. Superior force, divide and conquer."

Vyn rubbed the back of his head. "I wish I knew how many they have."

The kid shrugged. "More than seven."

"So..." Campion shifted. "Challenge single combat?"

All men turned. That was an interesting suggestion, a tactic they had used before.

Abrahim glanced at him. "And who would that be? You?"

"Me," said Campion.

Abrahim popped his neck. "Single combat isn't—"

"—an option," said Valerian. "Honor dictates you hold up your end of the bargain. If we lose, are we going to let them in to destroy the Elder Wood?" No man spoke. "So. No offer of single combat. Although I would like to see that, Campion, provided you won."

Campion smiled. "How could I not?"

Bantam glanced sideways. "Stahl, what are you doing?"

Stahl had removed most of his Armor, letting it bounce into the field. "My clothes are bugging me. They're not bugging you?"

"No."

"They're all jammed up."

Stahl continued to remove plate after plate.

Abrahim sighed and turned. "What did Twilight tell you about them?"

Valerian looked up to the mountains. "They're called trols. Big. Strong. Slow."

"Like Stahl," said Bantam. Stahl continued to strip off his plate and blew the kid a raspberry.

Valerian chuckled. "With trols, only males fight, only females use majik."

"Sorceresses," spat Abrahim. "I hate sorceresses."

"But no virago or valkyries," said Campion. "Czekna nearly killed you."

Abrahim squinted. "She got closest yet."

"Most trols are fighters," said Valerian. "I learned a few social protocols, proper forms of address. Some rituals. It's a culture based on strength. Might makes right." He turned to Abrahim. "Here's one you'll like: if you surrender in combat, an officer must render up a family member to be sacrificed to the victor."

Abrahim snorted, frowning. "Barbarians."

"Not quite. It's a rigid hierarchy, and there are rules. They worship dragonfire. I'm trying to think what else."

Abrahim turned. "Stahl, do you want me to get you a leotard?"

The mustachioed man dropped the last piece of armor to the ground and stripped off his shirt.

"You're going bareback?" asked Campion. "That chafes like hell."

"Not in *this* it won't." Stahl gestured to the titian Armor at his feet. "In fact—"

Stahl dropped his pants.

The reaction was immediate: loud cries of disgust followed by louder laughing. Bantam doubled over giggling. Even Valerian cracked up.

"No!" shouted Vyn.

Campion cackled. Abrahim too. Farrior started making that loud goose-honk he always made when he lost it.

Stahl loved that noise.

"I am not ashamed!" he yawped. "I no longer fear to stand naked before the world!"

Stahl placed his hand on his hip and struck the heroic pose of his statue. More laughing.

"If he's freeflapping, I'm leaving," said Abrahim, heading back for the arch.

Valerian followed, chuckling. Campion and the others trailed after, braying as they went.

Farrior stayed just long enough to finish another honk, his cheeks red. "You're an idiot, Stahl." He turned around to let the man change in peace.

Stahl wasn't having it. "Join me, my brothers! Join me in my freedom! Cast off your troubles and live as one with nature as God intended!"

He ran out of breath, chuckling.

It was always like this before a fight. *Screw around, lighten up. No point worrying about dying. Gonna happen sooner or later.*

Stahl stretched. They were out of earshot now and he let out a deep breath. *Good day. This is a good day.* He looked at the steel gleaming on the grass. *O, that Armor is outstanding.*

The danger of a siege was overthinking it. *Planning is for thin men with bad eyesight. You can plan to go to battle, but the battle won't go to plan. Best just meet it as it comes.*

He plonked the helmet on his head, enjoying the breeze between his legs.

I should walk back like this.

A *whomph* burst into existence behind him, followed by another and another in rapid succession. The *wikk* of it sizzled against his skin in painful ripples. The bursts of power in the air whipsnapped and melded together into one giant sound, and a blast of cold air hit him like a wave.

He ducked his head, reflexively protecting it despite the helm.

Sploff! Something hit his shoulder. It was cold on his bare skin. It fell apart, breaking, spattering to the ground in hunks. Stahl looked at it, his brain finally processing what it was.

Snow.

Turning, he brushed the clump off his shoulder. *Where did that come fro—*

A fat brown belly hung above his head.

Stahl took an involuntary step back as another wad of snow sloughed off the brown gut and splatted to the ground.

Giant tree-trunk legs stood on either side of him, supporting the belly. Above that, a chest like a barn door, hung with a necklace of skulls. Huge apelike shoulders, caked in snow. Above that, a long brown face with a series of nine horns embedded from the smallest near the eyes to the biggest at the end of its snout. The prime horn was five feet long, inlaid with gold etchings and rings dangling trinkets of metal and bone. The giant's fist gripped a dead tree as a club. It wore fur and smelled like a dead horse.

Three hundred more trols stood behind it.

Stahl stood before them buck naked.

O God. It's my nightmare.

Stahl eyed the giant's horns. That big one was filed sharp as a nail. He had a brief image of himself impaled on that horn, perhaps seconds from now. *Of all the moments to be caught with my pants down...*

"Hello!" Stahl said loudly, as if he were not completely nude.

Dark *wikk* sizzled the air around two she-beasts. They each held long blueflame staves in meaty hands. They smelled of burnt dragon. There were more women in the back, surrounding the raiding party in blueflame.

Is that how they ported in? Talk, idiot!

"I suppose you wonder," Stahl stalled, "why I should be here to greet you. In such a fashion. Today." A puff of air tickled his backside.

"Well." He gestured. "It is to show good... comraderies, ah, between warriors. A show of strength. To display our...fearlessness. It's traditional. But, seeing as all of *you* are clothed..." He bent and began buckling his plate to his loins. He glanced at the sabatons, the beautiful iron shoes he desperately wished he was wearing. *Doesn't matter. Running now would be suicide.* He glanced back up. The trol king hadn't moved, staring down at him with dark eyes.

Faster. Faster. His fingers worked quickly, expertly. *Talk!*

"Your arrival is most fortuitous. It is good we will have this time to... discuss together." He glanced over his shoulder. Too far away, his brothers were only beginning to realize what had happened. *Dammit, Farrior should be doing this dance, he's fantastic at wasting time with words. What would a courtier do? A* naked *courtier?* He belted on the codpiece. *Finally.*

Stahl looked up and found he had no need for deception.

"Wait, is that *part* of you?" Thick brown armored plates cascaded down the thing's shoulders and chest, its back and legs, the finest natural armor Stahl had ever seen in his life. The plates of skin were layered with tattoos, engravings, piercings, and patterned scarification. "That's your actual body? That's *spectacular*." His amazement was genuine, but his fingers continued their work. "What kind of piercing resistance do you get? An arrow couldn't even dent that. Probably not a spear either. You must be damn near invulnerable."

"Are you?" the leader grunted with a voice that rattled Stahl's teeth. The humongous club came away from its shoulder, swinging.

"*Ahh.*" Stahl snatched a vambrace and the dead tree hit him like a runaway carriage.

He flew forty feet backwards before he bounced against the ground, rolled backward twice, then dragged a ten-foot scar into the earth with his helmet.

Valerian was the first to reach him, followed closely by Farrior. "Stahl. *Stahl!*"

The helm rose slightly and Farrior heard a moan.

Stahl dragged himself painfully up to a sitting position. "I think we might be in trouble."

Valerian thumped him on the chest. "You're not dead. That's a good start." He looked up at the army of trols. "Hold the fort, would you?" he said and walked out to meet the enemy.

Stahl assessed his bruised body. Broken bones. At least one rib. From his waist to his ankles, he was covered by the elven aegis, and perfectly fine. His chest and arms, however, were bare as his pink toes, and savaged. He tapped Farrior, handing him the salvaged vambrace. "Help me get this on. My arm's broke."

The gigantic monsters chuckled. Their weird witcher-women stood, chanting incantations behind white-lidded eyes, keeping the flames burning. Valerian was shorter than the trol king, a quarter of its size, but still the man didn't seem small.

"I am Valerian Tsai. We protect these people now. There is nothing for you here. Depart in peace."

"Protect," laughed the giant trol king. "Little protection from little men. Paid dogs speaking for cowardly masters." It pounded its club into the ground. "Turn them out, little dog. Let them defend themselves. We will have what lies in that wood. We will have their majik."

"Turn back," said Valerian without pause. "Douse your flames and return to the Juttland. Your blood is too great to spend on this unworthy effort."

The beast lowered its head, eye to eye with the man. It snorted, puffs of steam blasting from huge nostrils on either side of Valerian. To his credit, the captain didn't flinch.

The thing stared him down. Neither of them blinked. The beast huffed, then glanced at the titian plate mail laying in the grass next to Stahl's sword. It thumped its club on it, burying steel beneath wood.

It smiled, showing broken teeth.

"Protect your elves, little man. I'll give you three minutes for not barking as a dog might. Three minutes to make peace with your God."

Valerian nodded sharply and turned. Abrahim leaned forward, bracing for the king to hit Valerian in the back, but the blow didn't come.

The brothers gathered around the half-naked Stahl. Valerian dragged him to his feet.

"You okay?"

"Mmf. Yeah. Good." Stahl grimaced. Two ribs, minimum. His chest was bleeding freely. *Probably my back, too, by the wet of it.*

"You're an idiot," said Campion.

"Yeah. I'm with you."

Bantam's voice piped up. "I didn't realize God *made* asses that wrinkly."

Vyn snorted and suddenly they all were laughing again.

"So," said Valerian. "Bit of a pickle."

"Without the rest of my Armor and my sword," Stahl said, grimacing, "I'm not going to be much good."

Bantam chuckled. "Of all the guys in the world to face down a horde naked…"

Farrior clamped the vambrace shut. Pain shot through Stahl as the bones of his forearm were pushed back into place. He managed not to yelp.

Abrahim shot air through his nose. "Do we center on the gate, or spread out over the entire wall?"

"There's a third option," Valerian said quietly.

Abrahim realized what the captain meant. A curled grin broke over his wizened face. "You're right. You're absolutely right."

"What?" Bantam looked around.

"We can't have Stahl *Shian* go into battle without armor," agreed Campion. "It just wouldn't be right."

"Besides," said Farrior. "I'm sick of looking at his nipples."

Vyn drew his bastard sword and grinned.

"Come on, Stahl." Valerian clapped him on one naked shoulder. "Let's get you suited."

A breath. A smile.

Seven men charged straight into the horde.

The trol king's eyes went wide. Some of the creatures took an involuntary step back. Together, the knights moved like lighting, faster than should be possible. Snarling, the king raised its club and howled. Warriors aped its movements and strode forward, closing the gap. When they met, the men faced a wall of monsters.

Stahl charged with them, pushing through the pain, weaponless; he didn't expect to survive the next moment.

Not a bad death.

A fusillade of clubs descended like hammers to a nailhead. Stahl had one moment to grit his teeth before they hit.

Their Armor flashed once.

> *A stroke of thunder without sound.*
> *A violent thump of wind. Time slows.*
> *Seven strokes of lightning land as one.*

Everything is turned away, away. Leather skin ripples, great
horns are smashed aside,
force smashing back every enemy,
away, away, away
Stahl watches a tree-club splinter into wooden shards around
Abrahim's body, never touching him. Campion radiates blood-
red light, sword flashing, eyes sharp behind steel. Farrior has
become an avenging angel,
shining golden.
Stahl feels himself, his powerful legs, his vambraced arm surging
with wonderous wikk, and he knows in that moment they can
defend against anything,
anything, anything.
Immovable as the earth, fixed forever.
And in their center, unbreakable bedrock.
Valerian.

Time snapped back into place as a thirty-foot crater surrounded them, smoking.

Through the haze, Stahl could see the giants reeling.

The seven men glanced at each other.

Good Lord Almighty.

"Did that just happen?" came Bantam's voice. He looked down at his breastplate, still sizzling indigo vapor.

Stahl stared at his right vambrace. Moonlit orange spilt through the ridges, glistening. The light shifted, waxing and waning.

The Armor. He looked at his brothers. *Not a mark on any of us.*

Outside the haze, a fierce bellow rose from the trol king. Stahl watched its long horn ignite in fire, five feet of flaming death. The blueflame torches rose and began their weirding dance.

"Stahl," Valerian's voice came.

Stahl didn't have any trouble finding his Armor. It was the only thing in the crater that wasn't destroyed, still gleaming brilliant orange.

The horde came.

Six men made a ring around him as Stahl dug up the plate. The onslaught hit and the battle was joined. Shouts, bellows, and clashing steel erupted around him.

Quick fingers clamped buckles shut.

Blueflame erupted somewhere in the haze and exploded over them. Blasted dirt and debris blazed with azure fire.

Vyn and Farrior kept their feet, barely.

"Stahl," growled Abrahim, dodging a fist big as a wagon wheel.

There was no time to don the sabatons. He'd have to go shoeless. Stahl buckled the breastplate over his bare chest. "Patience"—he picked up the rondels, strapping them, *one, two, three, four, five, six, seven locked*— "makes perfect."

He charged.

The battle was magnificent. All seven of them blazed strength and power.

An island against a sea of monsters.

Juttlanders fell two at a time. The paladin captain was the bulwark, driving into the largest wave, his brothers, the breakers. Stahl had never particularly enjoyed the thrill of combat, to him it was only a puzzle to be solved. But this moment, with the *wikk* coursing through him, dulling his pain with the roaring power of elven majik, was the closest thing to satisfaction he had ever known.

"Dammit." Abrahim's voice rang. "They're *smart*."

Stahl followed his eyes and saw a group of hulks cutting left toward the forest.

"I got 'em," came Vyn's voice and he broke left at a dead run.

"Bantam." Valerian jerked his chin. The kid took off sprinting after Vyn, then passed him.

Stahl glanced right. *Yep. They're smart.* More Juttlanders splitting off. Without a word, Stahl and Farrior went after them, leaving Valerian, Campion, and Abrahim to hold the center.

Stahl and Farrior ran together, quick as deer. Without clothing to crimp beneath it, Stahl's Armor fit like a second skin. His pink feet, however, had no defense against sticks and rocks. *Ow ow ow damn feet.* They caught up to the trols and hit them from the side, two against twenty.

Battle raged, the two men shifting between attack and defense. Old patterns fell into place and each man completed the other's moves, pulling one in and putting it down.

The bigger they are, the harder they fall was a saying Stahl always hated. *All lies. The bigger they are the harder it is to* make *them fall. Lord and Lady, these boys are huge.*

They played rope-a-dope with the second monster, but the third wasn't falling for it and smashed Stahl beneath the wagon it had been dragging.

The thing exploded, crushing him into the ground. Dust hung in the air.

From the wreckage, Stahl forced himself up. *Ow. Okay. Not invulnerable.*

Farrior drove the beast back, slashing its big brown belly. He glanced back at Stahl, driving the attack alone. "You really should be wearing boots for this."

Stahl grinned and got to his naked feet, standing side by side with his brother.

~⊹~

Bantam was everywhere. Vyn was a better fighter, but the kid was quick. While the jade knight took the brunt, the indigo tore the trols apart from the outside. Stahl watched the kid suddenly dart toward the center fight, toward Valerian.

Blueflame lashed from the giant crones, their staves radiating darkness. Explosions of earth and plumes of coldfire erupted around the knights in the center. The percussion wave hit Stahl from a hundred yards distant.

Debris clouded the skies and blotted out the center. All Stahl could see were the glowing colors of Armor through the haze. Purple moved toward the silver point—Valerian—then suddenly glowed brighter as the kid raced toward Stahl.

Stahl fended off an attack, slashing straight up between a Juttlander's legs as Bantam darted close to Farrior. "He says we can't hold them! Retreat to center and form ranks!" Then the kid was gone, heading back to Vyn.

"Good by me!" hollered Farrior.

Valerian, Campion, and Abrahim retreated toward the arch. It was no rout, not with *those* three fighting side by side, but the inevitability of it had begun. More coldfire explosions. Vyn and Bantam retreated as well.

Together, they pulled toward the...*do I call it a wall?* thought Stahl. *It's not a wall.* Stahl and Farrior skidded to a stop near the not-a-wall as more Juttlanders came at them. Stahl flicked a hand, his blood spraying the ground.

"So, these elves..." yelled Farrior.

"Yeah!" barked Stahl.

"They planned for this."

"Yeah!"

"They knew when we were coming. They knew when *these guys* were coming."

"Yeah!"

"So why is the bloody wall not done?"

"Well, there are always construction delays—"

A Juttlander grabbed Stahl by the waist and threw him through the wall.

White stone turned to powder, rock shattering everywhere. Orange light arced through the dust. Stahl's back struck a jagged boulder. He bounced and rolled in a jumble of plates.

Farrior's hand was there before his vision cleared. He hauled Stahl to his feet. "Try to stay up," he said as blood dripped from beneath his breastplate, and he was on the attack again, leveraging what remained of the wall as cover.

Stahl was with him. They held for a bit. The first monster got its knees taken out. The second was an easy target as it tried to come over its comrade. They scored a third. A fourth. There were more. Stahl's feet left bloody prints on the rock.

Inside the ward, the knights fell back. The trol king itself forced Campion, Abrahim, and Valerian through the half-finished arch. The three knights made the best of the kill zone for a time, leaving dead and wounded monsters in their wake, but soon the dam broke. The knights were forced in retreat to the center of the bailey.

Seven men back-to-back at the fountain. Giants came at them from every side.

Not a bad death.

Their Armor was caked in sweat and mud and blood. All of them were gasping for breath. Vyn was limping. Farrior's gut was bleeding. Campion had lost the use of his right hand and gone southpaw.

Only Valerian looked unhurt, straight as an arrow.

The trol king was slashed in a hundred places all along that thick hide. Still, it strode forward mercilessly, throngs of monsters in its wake. It stepped to the center of the courtyard and bellowed.

Valerian drove his blade into the stone at his feet.

The ring echoed through the courtyard, reverberating, painful and bright.

Valerian stared down the king with iron eyes. "Jarl Björn Glazier Vik-Kubiak, rightful heir to the Glazier Throne, second of his Riftline, King of Trol." Valerian's voice rang loud and sharp. "Look."

The burning horn of the beast tilted sideways, eyes never unlocking from the captain. It snorted. "You intend to win with trickery?"

"Look."

"Look at what, little dog?"

"Look around you."

Stahl looked, as did the king. Carnage. Ruin. The ward and the bailey were half-destroyed, the wall was broken. Smoke curled up from the burning wreckage beyond it.

"Look at your men."

The king turned. His soldiers were strong, but there were fewer now. Many lay in the trails of wounded, dead and dying behind him, in the ward, at the wall, and beyond it. A bloody smear of hulking corpses.

"Look at mine."

The seven knights stood at the fountain. As the trol king watched, their Armor glowed, thrumming with colored majik. The grime sizzled as it hissed away to ash and smoke. The paladins once again shone bright as new. Stahl felt the titian *wikk* coursing through his veins.

"We will fight you here at the fountain," said Valerian. "We will fight you at the wooden gate. We will fight you in the Elder Wood. And if one of us falls, we will still be six. And still, we will fight you. Every step you take forward will cost you another life. And we, the Border Knights, will fight to the last man standing. Yours or ours."

The trol king eyed the seven men.

"You may go deep into the Elder, O king," said Valerian. "But you will go alone. It will never be yours. How many more steps can you afford to take?"

Flames whickered at the horns of the trol king.

It tilted its head. "You have a proposal?"

"Relent," commanded Valerian. "The battleground is better defended than your women knew, and victory is not certain. Take your men and return to your mountain throne. And swear you will never return to the Elder."

The king frowned. "Never to return. Now, why should I do that?" came the deep voice, low and cold. "Why would I not come back with more men?"

"In return," said Valerian. "I will swear I will never bring these men to *your* home."

Stahl knew when it was time to flex. He snapped to attention and heard his brothers do the same.

He saw the expression on the beast's face. A hint of doubt. And something beneath that, far, far down. A touch of fear.

"You will make a gift to my people," the king demanded. "A sign of supplication."

Valerian Tsai took off his helmet. His black hair was plastered against his neck. Stahl imagined he saw just a bit of grey creeping in at the temples. The captain walked to the fountain and dunked his helmet in the water. Dripping, he walked straight toward the Trol King and presented the vessel.

"I offer you this water. I offer you health. I offer you life. I offer you peace."

Valerian tilted the helmet to his mouth and drank. He offered it to the king.

"Drink, Björn. And be satisfied to keep what you have."

A long moment.

Björn accepted the cup. He raised it, eyeing the grey man. Exhaling a long breath, he drank.

Bantam started to jump up and down in excitement. Abrahim put a firm hand on his shoulder before he could embarrass himself.

And then there was peace.

⁓

The horde returned to the field. As they did, curious elves emerged from the Elder. Flickering pillars of blueflame led the monsters away, and one by one the trol army began to shimmer in an eldritch glow.

Jarl Björn eyed the elves as one of the witcher-women apparated by his side in a flicker of black and blue fire.

"They are lucky to have you, Valerian Tsai." The king took a small package from her. "We would have torn through them like paper."

"Perhaps," said Valerian. "Perhaps not. Perhaps once you passed inside the Elder Wood, you would discover you had nothing left to want."

For a moment, they held eyes. "I doubt that." Björn held up the small package. "My gift."

"I forego my right," came Valerian's quick response.

"It is written by law."

"I do not want it."

"It does not matter what you want. This is the way it must be. My fortunes are large, and this is no loss to me."

"A third time, no."

Björn shrugged. "Then I will cast your gift to the mountain to be devoured by animals and be free of my burden." He reared back his arm to throw the thing over the wall.

"Stop," Valerian's voice rang. "I accept."

The king dumped the package on the ground at Valerian's feet and nodded to the witcher-woman. Her horns blazed blueflame and her eyes went white. The king's eyes, however, remained locked on the grey man.

"An honorable opponent, Valerian Tsai."

"An honorable opponent, King Glazier."

Something *whumphed* and they were gone, blue embers fading to nothingness.

Stahl let out a breath.

"That was a neat trick," said Bantam.

Valerian nodded, standing at the well. "No trick, just truth. What king wants to fight to the death?" Valerian filled the helmet again and drank deep. "A king has everything to lose. We are mere men."

He smiled and passed the bucket to Abrahim. The old man drank, wiping grit from his face, and passed the bucket to the next man. One by one they drank.

"Is that what I think it is?" asked the old badger, pointing at the abandoned package.

It was a little burlap sack, unadorned. It moved.

Valerian knelt beside it and untied the bag. The others gathered in.

Burlap fell away revealing a little brown hand, then an arm, then the stomach. The thing was mostly belly, and one little nub of a horn. Brown eyes blinked at them and it *boooed*.

Valerian picked it up. It reached out and touched his nose.

"That is the ugliest baby I've ever seen," said Bantam.

More elves appeared, arriving with food and bandages. The knights waved them off. They could bleed a few more moments together. The elven architects returned, moving back to their places on the wall, stones lifting slowly into place.

Stahl watched the elves work, taking a moment to breathe summer air.

The wall would be beautiful when it was complete, simple, elegant, and curved as a woman's hip. Looking at the incomplete arch, he raised a gauntleted thumb, closing the gap. The keystone over the top of the wall. He could see it there in the future, clear as day. The Arch.

Open. Huh.

He filled his helmet with water, drank, then dumped it over Farrior's head. Startled, Farrior sputtered. Everyone laughed. Abrahim's cackle, Campion's bray, Bantam's music, Farrior's honk.

His friends. His family. The best armor there was.

Stahl stood and walked away, his bare feet padding along the dirt.

"Where are you going?" shouted Farrior.

"Working perimeter. Get dinner started."

He slapped the bucket on his head, loving that it was already dry and clean.

And it fit him so well.

He passed through the Arch, taking first watch.

Not a bad life.

NOTE FROM THE AUTHOR

This was fun to write, I hope it was fun to read. I very much like the idea of the Border Knights, but never got the opportunity to let them all be together. When it came time to write a thank-you story for the readers of *The Legend of Black Jack*, the nature of the gift was never in question. Armor.

I'm with Stahl. Shoes are key. I couldn't care less about sunscreen or seat belts, but you won't catch me without shoes. My pink little piggies are vulnerable, and I mistrust coffee tables. I like the idea of telling the story of a guy who is so used to being under threat that he wears shoes inside his boots. Just in case.

In the end, it's not the Armor that's important. The thing that provides your best defense against the true dangers of the world is a group of people who love you. I hope you have met yours, and if not, I will be here until you do.

—A. R. Witham

ABOUT THE AUTHOR

A. R. Witham is a three-time Emmy-winning writer-producer and a great lover of adventure. He is the world's foremost expert on the history of Keymark. He loves to talk with young people and adults who remember what young people know. He has written for film and television, canoed to the Arctic Circle, hiked the Appalachian Trail, and been inside his house while it burned down. He lives in Indianapolis.

If you would like a sneak peek at his upcoming stories, please reach out to him:

arwitham.com

ALSO BY A. R. WITHAM

The Legend of Black Jack